Unless otherwise noted, all Scripture quotations are taken from the Holman Christian Standard Bible®, Copyright © 1999, 2000, 2002, 2003 by Holman Bible Publishers. Used by permission. Holman Christian Standard Bible®, Holman CSB®, and HCSB® are federally registered trademarks of Holman Bible Publishers.

Printed by CreateSpace, an Amazon.com Company

First Printing, 2016

ISBN 978-0692798287

www.walnutcreekchurch.org/wally

"Love the Lord your God with all your heart, with all your soul, with all your mind, and with all your strength.

The second is this: Love your neighbor as yourself. There is no other command greater than these."

Mark 12:30-31

B lue skies welcomed Wally to Oak Valley as he saw the yellow house for the first time. Their house stood out on the street of cut-and-paste gray boxes.

Wally had never moved before. He didn't know what to expect.

"Say hello to our new house! You are going to love this neighborhood," Dad said.

Wally and Claire waved to the house as they pulled in the driveway. Brightly colored tulips lined the walkway. A giant oak towered in the backyard, with a wooden treehouse right in the middle.

"This will be a fun adventure," Mom said.

Wally wondered what kind of adventure he would find.

All week Wally and Claire unpacked boxes with Mom and helped Dad paint the walls.

One day they played hide-n-go seek, exploring the new house for the best secret spots. After searching, Claire found Wally hiding in their room.

"Mom told me there are lots of kids who live on our street," Claire said. "Maybe we could ride bikes with them, or play baseball in the backyard!"

Wally didn't want to have a good attitude. He didn't feel at home. He missed their old

neighborhood and old friends. "I don't want to meet any new kids," Wally said.

"New things are always an adventure. Let's go find one!" said Claire as she tagged Wally and ran down the hallway. "Now, you're it!"

Claire thought if Wally could have fun, then maybe he would feel better and get excited about their new adventure. She always knew how to cheer Wally up.

In the blue house across the street lived a boy named Pablo. With his cape flapping behind him, Pablo flew down the stairs.

"Prepare for landing! I'm coming in!" said Pablo as he rounded the corner. "Super Pablo is here! And he is super hungry."

"Slow down there, superhero," said Pablo's mom. "These enchiladas are for the family that moved across the street, to welcome them to the neighborhood."

Pablo remembered a story he had read about Jesus in the Bible.

"That's like when Jesus tells us to love our neighbor as ourself. I think that means we should be kind to people and love people just like we would want them to be kind to us," Pablo said. "Is that right, mom?"

"You're right, bud. And Jesus wants us to obey His Word. The new family has a boy and girl right about your age," said Pablo's mom. "What would Super Pablo do to love them as his neighbor?"

The Bible says,

"**Love** the Lord your God with all your heart, with all your soul, with all your mind, and with all your strength.

The second is this: **Love** your neighbor as yourself. There is no other command greater than these."

Mark 12:30-31

Let's talk:

1. What could Pablo do to **welcome** Wally and Claire to the neighborhood?

2. Are there any kids who live near you? How can you **love** them as your neighbor?

3. What does it mean to **love** God with all your heart, soul, mind, and strength?

4. How can you **obey** this command?

Back across the street in the yellow house, Claire was thinking about Wally.

She had asked Wally to play outside, but he didn't want to come. Claire didn't know what to do. She really wanted to make new friends in their neighborhood.

"Mom, can we meet the boy who lives across the street?" asked Claire. "Wally doesn't want to come. I'm nervous to go by myself."

"I'll walk over there with you!" Mom said. "I want to thank Pablo's mom for bringing us dinner last night, too."

Claire felt nervous as she walked up to Pablo and his friend playing in the front yard. They kicked around a soccer ball, trying to score a goal between two trees. She asked God to help her be brave.

"Hi, my name is Claire," she said quietly.

"My family just moved here. We live across the street in the yellow house."

Pablo smiled. He was excited to meet her. "Hi, Claire! I'm Pablo, or you can call me Super Pablo. This is Annie, she lives on our street, too," Pablo said.

"Do you want to play superspeed soccer with us?" Annie said.

"Really, I can play with you?" asked Claire. Pablo and Annie surprised Claire. She didn't expect them to be so friendly.

"Of course! It's more fun to play together," Pablo said.

Now Claire had a big smile, too. Pablo knew inviting Claire to play with them was the right thing to do.

Claire played soccer with Pablo and Annie all morning. She couldn't wait to tell Wally about their new friends.

"Wally! Today I met Pablo and Annie, and they taught me how to play this really fun game! Come play with us!" Claire said.

"I'm reading. Maybe later," Wally said.

"You've been reading all day. Please come play. I miss you," Claire said.

Wally wished he would have gone with Claire to meet Pablo earlier. He was upset she had fun without him.

"I don't want to play. Go away," said Wally without lifting his eyes from the book.

Claire thought if she told Wally about the game he would want to come play. Wally being sad made Claire feel sad, too. She didn't know how to help him.

After Claire left, Wally stayed in his room thinking about what he had said. He knew he had hurt Claire's feelings.

Wally prayed and talked to God about what he had done.

"God, I made Claire sad because I was mean to her. I made a wrong choice. I wasn't trying to hurt her. I'm scared to make new friends. I'm nervous that they won't be like my old friends. I don't want to tell Claire that I'm lonely. Why is it so easy for her to make new friends? Help me to be brave and kind and to forgive Claire."

"What are you up to, bud?" asked Dad as he walked into Wally's room.

"Nothing." Wally didn't want to talk.

"Claire is in the backyard with Pablo and Annie. You should go outside and check it out." Dad said. "Pablo's mom asked if you would want to play on his baseball team. I could be your coach!"

Wally could tell Dad was trying to cheer him up, but he didn't feel very cheery.

"I hurt Claire's feelings. She won't want to play with me. I made a mistake," Wally said.

Dad smiled and gave Wally a big hug.

"God knows we make mistakes, and He still loves us," Dad said. "That's why God sent Jesus to die on the cross so that we would know how much He loves us. God's love and forgiveness frees us to be honest with Him and other people. Claire loves you, Wally. Let's go find her."

The Best News

The Gospel is the Good News that God loves the whole world, and you!

1   God Loves You

God made the whole world and all the people in it. He **loves all people**, and that includes you. God knows all about you—all the good and the bad—and He still loves you. God created you to be with Him forever.

"But You, Lord, are a compassionate and gracious God, slow to anger and rich in faithful love and truth."

Psalm 86:15

2   The Bad News

The bad news is that your sins—the icky things in your heart—separate you from God. Because God is holy and all good, He must punish sin. The best news is that God made **a solution for sin** and a way for you to be His friend.

"For all have sinned and fall short of the glory of God."

Romans 3:23

"For the wages of sin is death, but the gift of God is eternal life in Christ Jesus our Lord."

Romans 6:23

3 Jesus Died For You

The Bible tells us that Jesus is perfect and has never sinned. **Jesus died on the cross** to save you and was innocently punished for your sin. Jesus rose from the grave and conquered death to bring you back to God.

"Jesus told him, 'I am the way, the truth, and the life. No one can come to the Father except through me.'"
John 14:6

"But God demonstrates His own love for us in this: while we were still sinners, Christ died for us."
Romans 5:8

4 You Can Receive Jesus Now

If you believe in Jesus and have faith that He has truly died for you, He will **forgive** you and come live inside of you. God makes us totally new, giving us **joy and hope**. We get to live with Him forever in heaven.

"If you confess with your mouth, 'Jesus is Lord,' and believe in your heart that God raised Him from the dead, you will be saved. One believes with the heart, resulting in righteousness, and one confesses with the mouth, resulting in salvation."
Romans 10:9-10

Wally walked with Dad downstairs. He didn't want to go outside just yet. He watched the new friends play in the backyard through the window.

Pablo could tell Wally was nervous. He thought about how he could love Wally as his neighbor. Pablo had an idea.

"Hey, Wally! I'm making a giant sand tower. Can you help me out?" asked Pablo.

"I guess I can try," Wally said. Wally was thankful Pablo had invited him to play first. That made him feel a little braver.

Wally almost forgot about making Claire sad because he was having so much fun.

"I'm sorry I wasn't kind to you, Claire. I didn't mean to make you sad. I didn't think about how my words might hurt your feelings," Wally said.

"I forgive you, Wally. I was sad because you were sad," Claire said. "Pablo and Annie

were so nice to me. They showed me I didn't need to be afraid to make new friends!"

"You're right. It isn't fun to be alone. I think

Pablo and Annie will be really good friends," Wally said.

"The best of friends!" Claire said.

The four friends spent the blue sky afternoon running through the sprinkler and teaching Wally how to play superspeed soccer.

As the sun was setting over Oak Valley, the friends ate ice cream together in the tree behind the yellow house, remembering all the day's adventures.

"I'm happy that we're neighbors. This feels like home," said Wally as he smiled. He had an idea. "This treehouse could be our friendship headquarters!"

"Good idea, Wally. Let the fun begin!" Pablo said.

Walnut Creek Church is a vibrant
multi-site Christian community in the
greater Des Moines area. We have a desire
to love people practically and see all
develop a rich relationship with Christ.

www.walnutcreekchurch.org

About the Illustrators

Joel and Ashley Selby are a husband-and-wife illustration team who have worked side-by-side since meeting in a freshman drawing class in 2004. They maintain a unique style that carries across a wide spectrum of work: from colorful prints and cards in their online shop and retail stores, to illustrations for The Land of Nod and American Greetings. They run their freelance studio, This Paper Ship, from a converted former cotton mill in Saxapahaw, North Carolina, where they live with their daughter Sadie, four cats, piles of laundry, and art books. This is their first illustrated children's book.

Learn more about Joel and Ashley at www.thispapership.com.

About the Author

As a kid, Jackie Wallentin would read books with a flashlight under the covers long after bedtime. These late nights fostered a love of stories, both reading and writing them.

After intern adventures crafting words in the newspaper and marketing fields, Jackie graduated from Drake University with degrees in journalism and English. Now she uses a mix of both as a writer and designer at Walnut Creek Church in Des Moines, Iowa. When not working, Jackie enjoys spending as much time outside as possible, a good conversation, and any scoop of ice cream.

Made in the USA
Coppell, TX
08 October 2022

84282834R00021